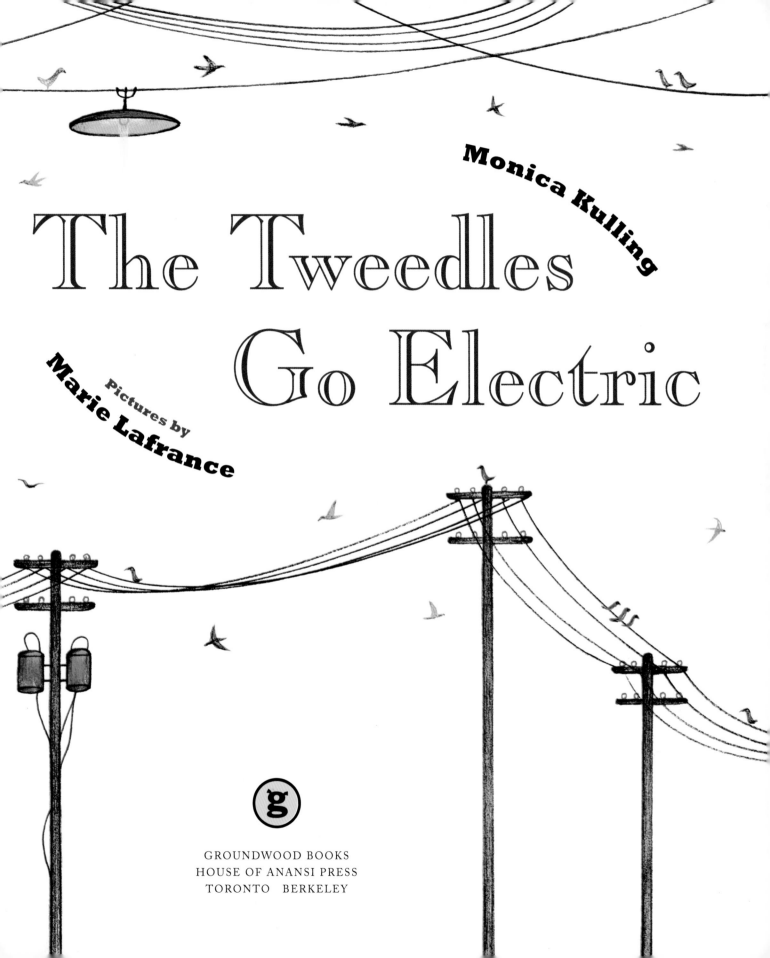

The Tweedles Go Electric

Monica Kulling

Pictures by
Marie Lafrance

GROUNDWOOD BOOKS
HOUSE OF ANANSI PRESS
TORONTO   BERKELEY

The Tweedles don't own a car. People think they're behind the times. Their neighbors, Mr. and Mrs. Hamm, are downright rude about it.

"You Tweedles are a bunch of fuddy-duddies," says Mr. Hamm whenever he sees them.

The Tweedles don't mind. They get around.
They walk or ride their safety cycles.
   There they are now — Papa, Mama, twelve-
year-old Frances and eight-year-old Francis —
all wheeling along on a summer's day.

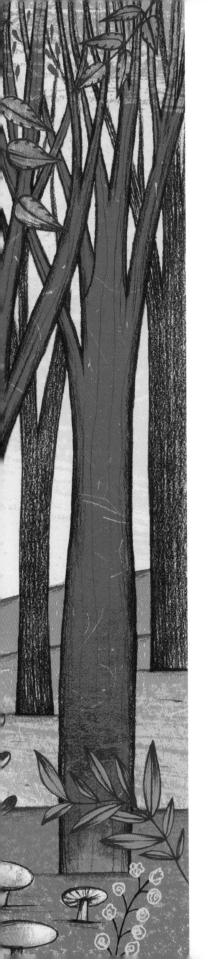

When the Tweedles need to go a distance, Papa hitches their horse, Mercury, to a cart. That's when they really travel at a clip.

But it's a new century. It's 1903!

One morning at breakfast, Papa makes an exciting announcement.

"We're going modern. We're buying a car!"

Mama's mouth flies open, but no words come out. She plunks the plate of teetering flapjacks on the table and starts to dance a jig. Secretly, Mama has always wanted a car.

Francis, or Frankie as his friends call him, shouts, "Yippee!" He grabs Mama's hands and the two of them dance together.

Francis, like most boys, loves adventure. And he loves wheels — scooters, cycles and wooden toy cars. Even the waterwheel at the flour mill is good for an afternoon of dreaming.

Wheels don't mean a thing to Frances, or Franny as her friends call her. Like most girls, she is more interested in higher education. Speed gives Frances nosebleeds, and adventure seems to go along with getting lost, which makes her nervous.

There's only one place Frances puts her nose and that is between the pages of a book. When she hears Papa, she doesn't even look up to ask, "What for?"

In these early years of the new century, most cars are powered by steam or gas.

Steam cars are unreliable. They might blow up in your face!

Gas cars are dirty and noisy, and they belch clouds of soot and smoke. Rattling down the road, they shake every tooth in your head — although that doesn't stop people from buying them.

But Papa has a different idea.

"We're going electric!" he says.
"Electric?" everyone shouts at the
same time.

Electricity is new and scary. People don't really understand it. They find it more frightening than a basket of boas.

Telephone lines in the city hang like bundles of vines in a jungle. No one with any sense stands under them for too long.

"Are electric cars safe?" asks Mama nervously.

"Safe as houses," replies Papa wisely.

"What does that mean, exactly?" asks Frances.
She has read that expression in a book somewhere
and doesn't understand it.

Papa doesn't either.

Frankie wants to know only one thing.

"Are they fast? Like a lightning bolt? *Zap!*"

Mama and Frances flinch. An electric car
sounds dangerous.

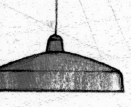

There is only one electric car at Mister Mo's Motors. It is green.

"The color of Mama's beautiful eyes," says Papa.

"The color of trees and grass!" says Francis.

"The color of money," says the ever-practical Frances.

"Why is there only one?" asks Mama.

"This car has an electric heart," replies Mister Mo, puffing on a fat cigar. "People don't want that. They want noise. They want smoke." *Puff! puff!* goes the cigar. "They want a car to sound and smell like a car."

"This is the car for us," says Papa. He lays down all the money he's saved from *not* owning a car. It comes to quite a stack.

"Hop in, everyone!" he shouts, happy as a clam at high tide.

Everyone piles in, and Papa starts the electric car. The engine purrs as he slowly drives the green car off the lot.

Mister Mo waves and puffs on his fat cigar.

"It's easy to drive!" he yells. "A kid could do it!"

Out on the road, the traffic is helter-skelter and every whichaway. There are no signs or lines. All kinds of wheels pack the road and go wherever they find a way.

There are gas cars and steam cars. There are cycles, and wheels pulled by horses. People walk, ride scooters, or push carts.

Suddenly a one-cylinder gasoline clunker pulls up. The driver honks and shouts, "Get a real car!"

Papa looks to see who it is, and wouldn't you know it. It's Mr. Hamm, the butcher, and his wife, Gladys.

"It's electric!" shouts back Papa. He thinks Mr. Hamm admires the electric car.

"It's green," shouts back Mama, smiling and waving.

"It's smart!" shouts back Francis, bouncing up and down.

Frances looks up from her book. "It's a car, Frankie," she says. "It can't be smart. It hasn't got a brain."

"But it's got a heart, Franny!" shouts Francis. "An electric heart!"

The Hamms roar off and leave the Tweedles in a cloud of black smoke.

Then a steamer rumbles by. One of the passengers leans out and shouts, "Get a horse!"

"We're electric," shouts back Papa, all smiles.

"We're green!" shouts back Mama, waving.

"We're smart!" shouts back Frankie, beaming.

Frances looks up from her book and rolls her eyes. She wishes she were at home, reading in peace.

"Faster!" yells Francis.

Papa pushes down the pedal. The humming increases, and so does the speed. The smart green car clicks along at ten miles an hour! They pass a woman on a penny farthing.

"Not *too* fast, Papa," warns Mama. "Remember Frances's nose."

"Which one?" asks Papa, concentrating.

"She only has the one nose, dear," replies Mama.

"I mean which Frances," says Papa. He swerves to avoid a horse and cart.

The next morning Papa cycles to work.

"I need time to get used to owning a car," he explains.

Mama, Frances and Francis are eating breakfast when someone bangs on the door.

Gladys is out of breath, and Mr. Hamm is holding his hand in a tea towel filled with ice. There is a look of pain on his face.

"The mare is sick," says Gladys, in tears. "Our car is out of gas, and Mr. Hamm has lopped off his finger! We need to get to the doctor fast, and you have that wonderful electric car."

"But no one here can drive," says Mama.

Frances puts down her book. She hears Mister Mo's parting words in her head. *A kid could do it!*

"I'll drive," says Frances. And she does. Everyone piles in the car. Frances steps on the pedal and zips down the road — all the way to the doctor.

Frances saves the day, and Mr. Hamm's finger.
Mr. Hamm is so grateful, he brings over his
best meats every week. He tells everyone the
Tweedles are smart for owning a reliable car.

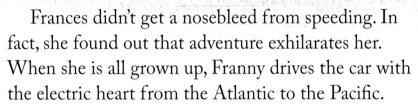

Frances didn't get a nosebleed from speeding. In fact, she found out that adventure exhilarates her. When she is all grown up, Franny drives the car with the electric heart from the Atlantic to the Pacific.

Frankie becomes a racing-car driver. And even Mama learns how to drive. Papa still rides his bicycle to work.

"I'm safer that way," he says, happy as a clam at high tide.

For Margaret Buffie and her granddaughter
Emily, early fans of the Tweedles, and for Nancy,
constant reader. — MK

To the magnetic Monica. — ML

Text copyright © 2014 by Monica Kulling
Illustrations copyright © 2014 by Marie Lafrance
Published in Canada and the USA in 2014 by Groundwood Books

Groundwood Books / House of Anansi Press
110 Spadina Avenue, Suite 801, Toronto, Ontario M5V 2K4
or c/o Publishers Group West
1700 Fourth Street, Berkeley, CA 94710

We acknowledge for their financial support of our publishing program the Canada
Council for the Arts, the Government of Canada through the Canada Book Fund
(CBF) and the Ontario Arts Council.

Canada Council **Conseil des Arts**
for the Arts **du Canada**

ONTARIO ARTS COUNCIL
CONSEIL DES ARTS DE L'ONTARIO

Library and Archives Canada Cataloguing in Publication
Kulling, Monica, author
The Tweedles go electric / written by Monica Kulling ; illustrated
by Marie Lafrance.
Issued in print and electronic formats.
ISBN 978-1-55498-167-0 (bound).--ISBN 978-1-55498-478-7 (html)
I. Lafrance, Marie, illustrator II. Title.
PS8571.U54T84 2014   jC813'.54   C2013-900384-3
C2013-900385-1

The illustrations were done in graphite on paper and mixed media collage,
then colored in Photoshop.
Design by Michael Solomon
Printed and bound in Malaysia